Winnie the Pooh
and the Blustery Day

$\boxed{p}$

Winnie the Pooh, or "Pooh" for short, lived with his friends in the Hundred-Acre Wood. One very blustery day, when the winds decided to stir things up, Pooh went to visit his thinking spot.

This book belongs to

_____

Characters (In order of appearance)
Narrator   LAURIE MAIN
Winnie the Pooh   JIM CUMMINGS
Tigger   EDWARD GILBERT
Christopher Robin   TIM HOSKINS
Gopher   MICHAEL GOUGH
Piglet   JOHN FIEDLER
Owl   HAL SMITH
Eeyore   PETER CULLEN
Rabbit   KEN SAMSOM
Kanga   PAT PARRIS
Roo   NICHOLAS MELODY

Editor   MARGARET ANN HUGHES
Producer   TED KRYCZKO
Engineer   GEORGE CHAROUHAS
Art Director   PAUL WENZEL

Hip Hip Pooh Ray (00:49)
Words and music by ROBERT B. SHERMANN
and RICHARD M. SHERMANN
© 1964 Wonderland Music Company Inc. (BMI)
The Wonderful Thing About Tiggers (00:48)
Words and music by ROBERT B. SHERMANN
and RICHARD M. SHERMANN
© 1963 Wonderland Music Company Inc. (BMI)
All rights reserved.
© 1963 & 1964 Wonderland Music Company, Inc. (BMI)
All rights reserved.
International © secured ℗ 2002 Walt Disney Records
© Disney
Based on the "Winne the Pooh" works by A.A. Milne
and E.H. Shepard
© Renewed. International © secured.
All rights reserved. Used by permission.

This is a Parragon book
First published in 2006
Parragon
Queen Street House
4 Queen Street
Bath BA1 1HE, UK

ISBN 1-40546-700-2
Manufactured in China

As Pooh sat there, trying hard to think of something, up popped his friend, Gopher. "Say, Pooh, if I were you, I'd think about skedaddlin out of here. It's Windsday, see?"

Pooh thought that sounded like a lot of fun. "Then I think I shall wish everyone a happy Windsday, and I will begin with my dear friend, Piglet."

The wind was blowing very hard as Pooh neared Piglet's house. "Happy Windsday, Piglet. I see you're sweeping leaves."

"Yes, Pooh. But it's hard. This is a very unfriendly wind."

Just then, a big gust blew Piglet up into the air. Pooh watched in surprise. "Where are you going, Piglet?"

"I don't know, Pooh. Oh, dear!"

Pooh tried to help, but when he grabbed Piglet's sweater, it began to unravel!

Piglet flew like a kite over the countryside, with Pooh dragging behind. The two went right through Eeyore's house and Rabbit's carrot patch.

Then with the blusteriest, gustiest gust of all, Piglet and Pooh were blown right up to Owl's house in a tall tree.

"Pooh! Piglet! This is a special treat! I so rarely get visitors up here. Do come in." Owl opened his window and in blew Pooh and Piglet.

The wind blew harder and harder until finally Owl's tree, along with his house, crashed to the ground. Everyone from the Hundred-Acre Wood came to help Owl, but only gloomy old Eeyore seemed to know what to do. "If you ask me, and nobody has, I say when a house looks like that, it's time to find another one. A thankless job, but I'll find a new one for him."

And off he plodded.

Finally, the blustery day turned into a blustery night.

To Pooh, it was an uncomfortable night full of uncomfortable noises. And one of the noises was a sound he had never heard before. "Gr-r-r-rol!"

Pooh got up and went to his door to investigate. "Hello, out there! Oh, I hope nobody answers."

Just then a funny looking animal bounced into the room.

"Hi, I'm Tigger. T-I-double Guh-ER."

Pooh put down his pop-gun. "You scared me."

"Sure I did! Everyone's scared of Tiggers!"

"Well, what's a Tigger?"

"Glad you brought that up, chum!"

Then Tigger bounced around the room to show Pooh
what a Tigger was.

Tigger stopped bouncing. "Did I say I was hungry?"

"Not for honey, I hope."

"Yuck! Tiggers don't like that icky, sticky stuff. Well,
I better be bouncing along. T.T.F.N.! Ta-ta for now!"

The wind continued to blow. There was a clap of thunder and it began to rain. And it rained, and it rained, and it rained.

By morning, the Hundred-Acre Wood was flooded.

Pooh tried to rescue his honey by eating it all for breakfast. He was upside-down, licking the bottom of the last pot, when the water floated him right out his front door.

At Piglet's house, the water was coming in through the window. He wrote a message and put it into a bottle. The message read, "Help Piglet (Me)". The bottle floated out of his house and out of sight.

Christopher Robin lived high on a hill where the water couldn't reach. So that was where everyone from the Hundred-Acre Wood gathered. Before long Christopher Robin discovered Piglet's bottle and read the message. "Owl, fly over to Piglet's house and tell him we'll plan a rescue."

As Owl flew over the flood, he spotted two tiny objects below. One was Piglet, standing on a chair, and the other was Pooh, still upside-down in his honey pot. Owl called down to them and told them of the rescue.

"Be brave, little Piglet!"

"Thank you, Owl, but it's awfully hard to be brave when you're such a small animal."

Pooh and Piglet eventually floated to the very spot where Christopher Robin was waiting.

"Pooh, you rescued Piglet! That was a very brave thing to do. You're a hero!"

"I am?"

"Yes. And so I shall give you a hero party!"

Just as the hero party began, Eeyore arrived with news.

"I found a house for Owl. If you wanna follow me, I'll show it to you."

Eeyore led them through the woods and, to everyone's surprise, stopped in front of Piglet's house. "This is it."

Pooh tried to convince Piglet to speak up.

"No, Pooh. This house belongs to our good friend, Owl. I shall live...shall live..."

"You shall live with me." Pooh put his arm around his little friend.

Christopher Robin was especially proud. "That was a very grand thing to do, Piglet – giving your house to Owl."

And so, the one-hero party became a two-hero party. Pooh was a hero for saving Piglet's life and Piglet was hero for giving Owl his grand home in the beech tree.

Hip Hip Hooray!

Winnie the Pooh
and Tigger Too

Winnie the Pooh lived in an enchanted place called the Hundred-Acre Wood. One day, while he was thinking in his thoughtful spot, he was bounced by a springy character with stripes.

"Hello, Pooh. I'm Tigger! T-I-double Guh-ER!"

"I know. You've bounced me before."

Tigger liked to bounce, especially on unsuspecting friends. Piglet was sweeping leaves when Tigger bounced him. All the leaves went flying.

"Hello, Piglet! That was only a little bounce, you know. I'm saving my best one for Rabbit." And Tigger bounded over to Rabbit's house.

Rabbit was happily working in his vegetable garden when Tigger called out a greeting. "Hello, Long Ears!"

"No, no, Tigger! Don't bounce...!"

But Rabbit couldn't stop Tigger from bouncing. Vegetables went flying in all directions.

A very discouraged Rabbit sat down on the ground.
"Tigger, just look at my beautiful garden."

"Yuck! Messy, isn't it?" Tigger frowned in disgust.

"Messy? It's ruined! Oh, why don't you ever stop
bouncing?"

"Why? That's what Tiggers do best!" And off Tigger
bounced down the road.

Rabbit was so upset about his garden that he called a meeting at his house, which Pooh and Piglet attended.

"Attention, everybody! Something has got to be done about Tiggers bouncing. And I have a splendid idea. We'll take Tigger for a long explore in the woods and lose him. And when we find him, he'll be a more grateful Tigger, an 'Oh, how can I ever thank you for saving me' Tigger. And it will take the bounces out of him."

It was agreed. The next morning, Pooh, Piglet and Rabbit took Tigger for an early misty-morning walk in the woods. Tigger bounced up ahead.

Then, when Tigger wasn't looking, Rabbit, Pooh and Piglet hid in a hollow log.

It wasn't long before Tigger noticed he was alone. "Now where do you suppose old Long Ears went to? Hallooo! Where are you fellas? Gee, they must have gotten lost."

And Tigger bounced off to find his friends.

When all seemed clear, Rabbit crept out of the log and called the others to join him.

"You see? My splendid plan is working! Now we'll go and save Tigger."

But as they walked on, they kept coming back to the same sandpit. Pooh, who is a bear of very little brain, had a thought. "Maybe the sandpit is following us, Rabbit."

"Nonsense, Pooh. I know my way through the forest." And Rabbit left to prove he could find his way home.

After Rabbit had been gone awhile, Pooh felt a rumbling in his tummy. "I think my honey pots are calling to me. Come on, Piglet. My tummy knows the way home."

Just then, who should appear but Tigger. He happily bounced Pooh and Piglet. "I thought you fellas were lost!"

It turned out that the only one who was lost was Rabbit!
All alone in the dense woods, he jumped at every noise.

Rabbit grew more and more frightened. The thick mist
was filled with strange shapes and sounds.

Suddenly, he heard "Hallooo!" Before he knew it, Rabbit
was found, and bounced, by an old familiar friend.

"Tigger! But you're supposed to be lost!"

"Oh, Tiggers never get lost, Bunny Boy. Come on, let's
go home."

Rabbit took hold of Tigger's tail, and Tigger bounced
him all the way home. This time, Rabbit didn't seem to
mind a bit.

Before long, winter came and transformed the Hundred-Acre Wood into a playground of white fluffy snow. Roo was so anxious to play with Tigger that his mother, Kanga, barely had time to tie a scarf around his neck. "Have him home by nap time, Tigger."

"Don't worry, Mrs Kanga. I'll take care of the little nipper."

Then off they bounced, because that's what Tiggers and Roos do best!

Soon, they came upon a frozen pond where Rabbit was skating gracefully on the ice. Roo watched in amazement.

"Can Tiggers skate as fancy as Mr Rabbit?"

"Sure, Roo. Why, that's what Tiggers do best!"

But when Tigger ran onto the ice, he slipped and skidded right into Rabbit, and they all went crashing right through Rabbit's front door!

Tigger groaned. "Tiggers don't like ice-skating!"

Tigger and Roo looked for something else that Tiggers do best. Roo had an idea. "I'll bet you could climb trees, Tigger!"

"Tiggers don't climb trees. They bounce 'em!"

So Tigger and Roo bounced all the way to the top of a tall tree. Suddenly, Tigger realised just how far down the ground actually was. "Whoaa! Tiggers don't like to bounce trees!"

Roo, however, thought this was great fun. He swung back and forth, holding onto Tigger's tail. "Wheee-ee!"

"Stop, kid! S-T-O-P! You're rocking the forest!"

While Tigger was up in the tree, Pooh and Piglet were down below, tracking footprints in the snow. Piglet asked Pooh what they were tracking.

"I won't know until I catch up with it."

Just then, Pooh and Piglet heard a sound in the distance. "Hallooo!"

Pooh turned to his friend. "I hope it isn't a fierce jagular. Because they 'Hallooo' and then drop on you."

But it wasn't a jagular at all. It was only Tigger and Roo up in the tree.

Pooh looked up. "How did you and Tigger get way up there?"

"We bounced up!"

"Well, then, why don't you bounce down?" Pooh was very smart for a bear of very little brain. And so, Roo bounced down.

But Tigger was still too frightened to jump that far.

"Somebody, help!"

It wasn't long before word got to Christopher Robin that Tigger was in trouble.

Everyone quickly came to his rescue, but no one knew what to do. So I stepped in to help. "You see, Tigger? All your bouncing has finally gotten you in trouble."

"Who are you?"

"I'm the narrator."

"Oh. Well, narrate me down from here. If you do, I promise I'll never bounce again!"

So I turned the book sideways, and Tigger slid right down the block of type to land safely on the ground.

Tigger was most relieved to be on solid ground again.

"I'm so happy, I feel like bouncing!"

Rabbit crossed his arms. "No, Tigger. You promised!"

"You mean, not even one teensy-weensy bounce?"

When Rabbit shook his head, Tigger turned and walked away.

Roo tugged at Kanga's arm. "Mama, I like the old bouncy Tigger best."

And everyone agreed. So they gave Tigger his bounce back and he leaped for joy. Even Rabbit had to admit it. "Yes, I quite agree. A Tigger without his bounce is no Tigger at all".

The Wonderful Thing about Tiggers